Quack the Duck's Family

Written by Michèle Dufresne • Illustrated by Tracy La Rue Hohn

PIONEER VALLEY EDUCATIONAL PRESS, INC.

Here is my mom.
My mom is singing.

Here is my dad.
My dad is flying.

Here is my brother.
My brother is jumping.

Here is my sister.
My sister is walking.

Here is my grandpa.
My grandpa is sleeping.

Here is my family.
My family is swimming.